MW01045393

POMODORO PENGUIN AND tHE GEOGRAPHY GIRAFFE

The Adventures of Pomodoro Penguin, No. 2

by Bryce Westervelt

OPERA GOBBLER BOOKS~TM~

Pomodoro Penguin and the Geography Giraffe is a work of fiction. Names, characters, places, and events are either the products of the author's imagination or used in a fictitious manner. Any resemblance to actual persons, penguins, or other creatures -living or dead- as well as actual events is purely coincidental.

Copyright © 2014 by Bryce Westervelt
Published by Opera Gobbler Books, Centereach, New York

All rights reserved. No portion of this book may be reproduced, distributed, or transmitted in any form or by any means - electronic, mechanical, photocopying, recording, or otherwise - without written permission of the publisher.

Opera Gobbler Books publishes books in several electronic formats. Some content that appears in print may not be available in the electronic editions.

Library of Congress Control Number: 2013922995

ISBN   978-1-941047-03-3 (pb)
        978-1-941047-07-1 (mobi)
        978-1-941047-08-8 (epub)

Layout and interior design by Bryce Westervelt

Please send inquiries, correspondence, and fan mail to:
Pomodoro Penguin
c/o Opera Gobbler Books
PO Box 1376
Selden, NY 11784

www.PomodoroPenguin.com

Printed in the United States of America

First printing: March 2014

To Joshua, Moriya, and Kiernan

ALSO AVAILABLE:

Pomodoro Penguin Makes a Friend

Pomodoro Penguin Visits Italy

Pomodoro Penguin: Penguins, Penguins All Around

*Pomodoro Penguin and the
Halloween Costume Conundrum*

One sunny Tuesday,
on swings side by side,
the penguin and owl
played together outside.

Pomodoro and Violet
were swinging away.
The owl started yawning
and then turned to say:

"This swing is a bore.
I'm starting to snore.
Why don't we go
to the park to explore?"

"May Violet and I
walk down to the park?"
"Sure," said mom,
"but be back before dark."

Away to the park
the pair of birds sped –
the lavender owl
and the penguin who's red.

They played hide-and-seek
underneath an oak tree,
when Pomo saw something.
"Oh, what could that be?"

From the ground it looked round,
a bright colorful bubble!
It glowed and it buzzed!
This thing might be trouble!

"Getting it down
should be really easy.
Owl fly up there,
since heights make you queasy!"

"Okay," said Pomo,
"if that makes you happy.
Just do it quickly!
Go on! Be snappy!"

"THIS is like nothing
that I've ever seen.
It's a beautiful ball
of brown, aqua and green."

Violet approached
the branch high above.
She nudged at the ball
and then gave it a shove.

It started to buzz!
It started to stir!
It zoomed from the tree,
with a whiz and a whir!

This glowing ball
didn't monkey around!
It zipped right past Pomo
and fell to the ground!

Once it had landed,
they crept near the sphere.
"What a cool ball –
it's the toy of the year!"

While they admired
the ball all aglow,
A giraffe wandered by
with his head hanging low.

His eyes filled with tears,
he started to cry.
He sniffled and sobbed,
and let out a sigh:

"Where did I put it?
Oh, where did it go?
I've looked way up high
and I've looked way down low."

Then the big beast
stumbled into the owl.
She looked annoyed –
on her face was a scowl.

"Can we help you?" asked Pomo.
"Hey, you! Look down here!
Perhaps we could help you.
Say, what's with that tear?"

"I've lost my glasses –
I really can't see.
I can't find my globe
for geography!"

"Are those your glasses
on top of your head?
Perhaps they'd work better
on your eyes instead!"

"Oh, that's much better,"
said the tall giraffe.
"Thank you so much.
My name is Falstaff."

"Pleased to meet you Falstaff,
now that our paths have crossed.
I'm Pomo, she's Violet –
what else have you lost?"

"I'm sorry to bug you –
I don't mean to probe!"
Falstaff Giraffe asked,
"Have YOU seen my globe?"

"What's a globe?" asked Pomo
in a quizzical tone.
"What should we look for?
Is it like a calzone?"

"A globe is a map
that is shaped like a ball,
showing oceans and countries –
but that is not all!

MY globe is special –
it's full of magic.
That I've misplaced it
is really quite tragic!"

"Is this your globe that
we found in the tree?
Is THIS what you lost?
Could it be? Could it be?"

"Ah! YOU found my globe!
I'm one lucky guy!
I must have left it
up there, way up high!"

"Hoot, Hootie, Hooo –
will you share it with us?
Please show us your globe
if it isn't a fuss."

"I'd love to," said Falstaff.
"Let's give it a try.
I just ask it questions
like 'What?', 'Where?', or 'Why?'."

"It's getting late.
How long will this last?
Can you ask the globe quickly?
The sun's setting fast!"

"Oh, this will be quick!"
With a wink and a nod
Falstaff Giraffe bellowed,
his voice sounding odd!

"Magic Globe, Wondrous Globe –
my question seems daffy.
What is this thing you call
GEEE - OOOH - GRAPH - EEE?"

All of a sudden,
the globe started to smile –
with a grin as wide
as a country mile!

"Geography you ask?
What a fun little ditty!
Would you like a quick answer,
or the real nitty-gritty?"

"Magic Globe, it's late –
and they're in a hurry.
Please make it quick
so their mothers won't worry!"

"Geography's the study
of OUR planet -Earth.
I'm a miniature Earth,
for whatever that's worth."

"When you look at a globe,
there are oceans and land,
tall mountains, low valleys –
now isn't that grand?"

"There are countries and cities
and people and places –

- You seem quite amazed
by the looks on your faces!"

"Oh, wow!" said the penguin,
"There's so much to see!
You'll never get bored
learning geography!"

Then he asked Falstaff,
"If it's okay with you,
May Violet and I
learn geography, too?"

"Of course, little Pomo –
I'm here every week!
Just me and my globe
hanging out by the creek!

'Til then, little penguin,
see you later, good-bye!
The next time you're here,
please, be sure to swing by!"

"We'll see you next time
for geography classes.
Hopefully then
you'll still have your glasses!"

The new friends all smiled
and started to laugh.
Pomodoro and Violet
and Falstaff Giraffe.

CPSIA information can be obtained at www.ICGtesting.com
Printed in the USA
BVOW11s2317041115

425777BV00016B/189/P

9 781941 047033